POSTCARD

THE ADDRESS TO BE WRITTEN ON THIS SIDE

Thank you all so much if you took part in the doodle competition. It was so hard to choose a winner – they were all brilliant. **WELL DONE!**

WINNER!

KT-376-438

Daisy, 8, Peterborough

Runners Up

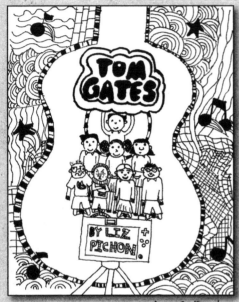

Ava, 9, London

Oscar, 8, Todmorden

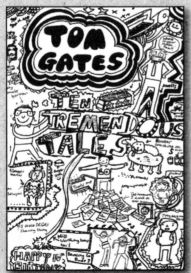

Laila, 14, London

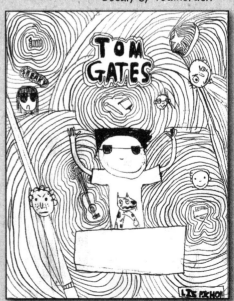

Theo, 8, Gloucestershire

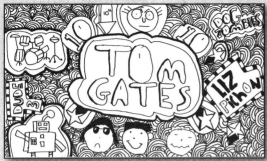

Euan, 11, Stockport

Ayaan, 9, Bromley

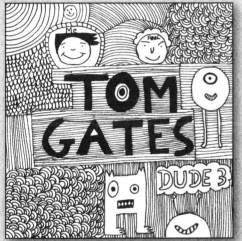

Stasha, 10, India

Ayaan, 9, Bromley

Iyla, 7, Eastbourne

QUIZ
There are doodles from the
VERY FIRST Tom Gates book
– THE BRILLIANT WORLD OF
TOM GATES – on the title
page of every story.
Can YOU spot them all?

TEN TREMENDOUS TALES

By Liz Pichon

SCHOLASTIC

Published in the UK by Scholastic Children's Books, 2021
Euston House, 24 Eversholt Street, London, NW1 1DB, UK
A division of Scholastic Limited.

London – New York – Toronto – Sydney – Auckland
Mexico City – New Delhi – Hong Kong

SCHOLASTIC and associated logos are trademarks and/or
registered trademarks of Scholastic Inc.

ISBN 978 0702 30252 7

A CIP catalogue record for this book is available from the British Library.

Printed by CPI Group (UK) Ltd, Croydon, CR0 4YY
Papers used by Scholastic Children's Books are made
from wood grown in sustainable forests.

1 3 5 7 9 10 8 6 4 2

www.scholastic.co.uk

POSTCARD

Hello, readers,

BLIMEY, time's gone super fast and it's been ten years since the first Tom Gates book came out in 2011. Thank you SO much to all the people who have helped to make the books, sold the books and read them. (That's YOU, by the way!) Did you know Tom is based on me as a kid? I loved drawing and caramel wafers, and I used to make toast doodles too. I hope you enjoy this book – I had fun making it.

Keep in touch!

Much love,

Liz xxxx

Lizpichon.com

1

Tremendous Tank Top

School's been a bit TRICKY for me this week because I keep forgetting things. (There's a LOT going on, so it's not ALL my fault.)

The first thing I forgot was when Mr Fullerman said,

> **THE QUICK-FIRE SPELLING TEST**

> Are you ready for the quick-fire spelling test?

I kept what I thought was a nice, relaxed expression on my face. But Marcus, who was sitting next to me, said,

"Ha! You forgot about the spelling test, didn't you?"

"NO, I've been practising," I replied.

(I hadn't.)

"Ignore him..." AMY told me.

Ha!

SOMEHOW, I managed to get through

the test by using a combination of

SUPER GOOD SKILLS:

① My sneaky side-eye spying (heavily

disguised as serious THINKING).

② Actually knowing how to spell SOME of

the words (which was unusual for me). ☺

So, in the end I didn't do too badly – but it was

touch and go. Phew

Then, the next day, Mr Fullerman came into class

and said,

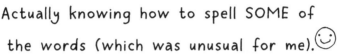 **Good morning, Class 5F!**

Everyone replied apart from me, because I'd been

THINKING about an **ADVERT** I'd seen

on TV the night before.

Suddenly I heard myself SAYING...

③

"Who's **MR SUNSHINE?**" AMY asked.

"I mean Mr Fullerman!"

I corrected myself, but it was TOO LATE.
The class started to LAUGH. HA!HA!HA!HA!HA!

Even Mr Fullerman was smiling. I felt like I had
to explain who **MR SUNSHINE** was, so I BLURTED out,

"It's from an **ADVERT! MR SUNSHINE** makes
people happy when they book a holiday.

The TUNE on the advert really sticks in your head, sir," I added.

"MR SUNSHINE isn't the worst thing I've been called," Mr Fullerman told me.

It took a while for the class to calm down. Even AMY laughed, but Marcus went RIGHT over the top and was doubled over in HYSTERICS.

"It wasn't that funny, Marcus," I told him.

"It ... Ha! Ha! HA! ... really ... Ha! Ha! ... was."

Then he stopped laughing because he got a stitch.

"It's your fault," he told me. (It wasn't.)

At least the stitch calmed him down though. Ohh.

5

Mr Fullerman stood at the front of the class and started CLAPPING out a rhythm to get our attention. We clapped back.

"If ANYONE has forgotten their dinner money or PACKED LUNCH today, put up your hand NOW, please."

I HAD my packed lunch, so there was no need to put MY hand up.

(Or that's what I THOUGHT.)

TEN MINUTES before the bell went for lunch, I realized my packed lunch was AT HOME.

When I told Mr Fullerman, he sighed.
"QUICKLY – go and tell the office so they can add you to the list for a free meal today. Otherwise you won't get any lunch.

But DON'T run!" he said in a weary voice.

I did my excellent ═══SPEED

walking all the way to Mrs Mumble,

who raised her eyebrows at me.

"OK, Tom, I'll put you on the lunch list. Please don't forget to bring in your money tomorrow."

I nodded. "Shall I email your parents just in case?" she checked.

"No need, Mrs Mumble - I will bring it in,"

I told her confidently.

When I got back to class, Mr Fullerman said EXACTLY the same thing! It was like no one believed I would remember.

"Shall I give you a note, Tom?"

"I REALLY won't forget, sir..." I assured him.

I sat down and AMY smiled while Marcus pulled a FACE. (That was annoying.)

"What's the FACE for?" I asked.

"You WILL forget your dinner money,"

he said smugly.

"No, I won't – look, I'm going to write it down in my notebook."

"And then you'll forget your notebook. You've been forgetting a lot of stuff lately, Tom – just saying," he added.

(The WORST thing about Marcus telling me that was ... I knew he was RIGHT.)

"I'm not THAT bad," I muttered under my breath.

"You are – I lent you my pencil the other day and you FORGOT to give that back too – OR you've lost it. So, I'll need another pencil. It was my FAVOURITE pencil," Marcus told me and folded his arms.

8

(Normally I wouldn't have asked him for ANYTHING, but my pencils were blunt from doodling.

It was an **EMERGENCY.**)

I <u>DID</u> still have his pencil, so I took it out of my case and gave it back.

"Here it is, Marcus. Thanks for lending it to me."

Marcus took the pencil and checked it over like I'd DONE something to it.

He got out some paper and wrote,

THIS PENCIL IS <u>MINE.</u>

"It's not very *SHARP*," he grumbled.

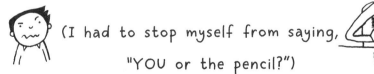

(I had to stop myself from saying,

"YOU or the pencil?")

I watched as Marcus began to **CHEW** the end of his pencil.

Which was

GROSS.

"Marcus, I wouldn't put that in your MOUTH if I were you," I told him.

"Why not? I can do what I want. It's MY pencil," he said smugly.

"THAT'S what I told Rooster when he picked it up," I whispered.

I was joking, but it made Marcus stop.

Then **AMY** *LEANED* forwards and said,

    "Hey, Marcus, that reminds me – YOU forgot to give me my ruler back."
Marcus looked SUSPICIOUS, like he wasn't convinced he had it.

"Hmmph... Are you SURE? Let me check,"
he grumbled and started rummaging
through his bag. Sure enough, Marcus
found the ruler.
He took it out and told **AMY**,

    "THIS ruler looks like mine.
      I don't think it's yours."

 **AMY** wasn't happy.

"Yes it is, Marcus. It's got my name on it," she told him.

"Where? I can't see it."
Marcus wasn't being very helpful.

"Just give it back, please," AMY said, getting annoyed, and she reached out to take it.

Marcus moved away.
Things were getting **TENSE** and I was stuck in the middle of them arguing over a ruler.

"Look – AMY's name IS on the ruler, SEE? Who's got a BAD memory now, Marcus?"
I said, pointing out AMY's name. Reluctantly, Marcus handed the ruler back.

He even said sorry (quietly).

"Well, Tom – you still forget WAY more things than I do, like your homework and your packed lunch."

Marcus HAD to go and remind me of that again. I was wondering what I could say BACK to him when I got distracted by a WAFT of school dinner cooking smell that had crept into our classroom.

(It was a nice smell, in case you were wondering.)

I tried to guess what it was by sniffing the air. Roast potatoes? Maybe it could even be one of my favourite lunches ...

... CHICKEN PIE, which was EXCITING.
"I think forgetting my packed lunch was a GOOD
thing, because whatever's cooking smells DELICIOUS.
So now I get to eat that instead,"
I told Marcus, making the POINT that, sometimes,
forgetting things CAN work out for the BEST.

Only this time, I was WRONG.
(VERY wrong.)

When the bell went for dinner, I rushed to the hall and it quickly became clear there was NOTHING on offer that I wanted to eat.

More kids started lining up behind me as I tried to work out WHAT food had smelt so nice.

"Come on, quickly, there's a queue building up,"
      the school cook told me.

I was under pressure to make up my mind.

"Um... Not the mince, it looks grey. Or the fish pie with the lumpy potato... I don't know," I muttered.

"Hurry up, we're hungry!" one of the kids called out.

"I'm **THINKING!**" I told them.

"**THINK FASTER!**" they said.

The cook told me to stand to one side and let the kids go in front. Then as I tried to decide, more and more kids went past, until I was right at the

 BACK of the queue.

That's when I noticed a new tray of food had been brought out. I couldn't quite see what it was, but I recognized the lovely smell.

And then I heard someone say...

"I'll HAVE THE CHICKEN PIE, PLEASE."

I nearly dropped my tray!

"CHICKEN PIE! THERE's CHICKEN PIE?"

I repeated.

This was exactly what I wanted.

I tried to rejoin the queue where I'd left it.

But the little kids wouldn't let me.

"NO PUSHING IN!" they all told me.

"I'm just reclaiming my PLACE! I know what I want

to eat now," I tried to explain.

Mr Sprocket came over to see what all the QUEUE JOSTLING was about.

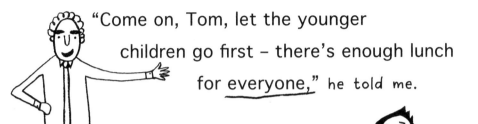

"Come on, Tom, let the younger children go first – there's enough lunch for <u>everyone</u>," he told me.

I had to wait my turn while EVERY SINGLE KID IN FRONT OF ME ASKED FOR ...
CHICKEN PIE.

All I could HEAR from the back of the queue was:

I'll have chicken pie, please.

Chicken pie for ME!

Chicken pie here too, please.

Chicken pie, please!

"SOMEONE, PLEASE HAVE THE MINCE OR THE FISH PIE - ANYONE! PLEASE LEAVE ME A CHICKEN PIE!"

I said loudly so that my desperation would be heard.

I edged closer and closer and kept muttering, "Chicken pie... Please, chicken pie... Please, chicken pie..." over and over again to keep me going. Until

☆ FINALLY, ☆

I got to the front and said,

AT LAST, CHICKEN PIE, PLEASE!

"**S**orry, they were very popular and all the pies have gone. But I've got tuna pasta if you want some?" the school cook told me.

(I did not want tuna pasta – no thank you very much.)
"Are you SURE they're all gone?" I asked her just in case.

"Yes – now what do you want instead?"

Reluctantly, I went for the mince and peas because I didn't really have much choice.

Walking past all the kids that were eating their chicken pies gave me SERIOUS food envy. I sighed a LOT.

I found a seat next to **N**orman and sat down.

"This chicken pie is DELICIOUS!"
was the first thing he said.

(BRILLIANT – not in a good way.)

"**T**HAT'S what I wanted," I told him sadly.

"Here, you can have a bit of my pie crust.

I'm STUFFED," Full!

Norman said and put a **BIG** piece on my plate.

Which tasted much better than my mince.

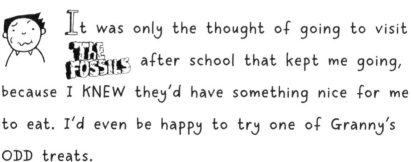

It was only the thought of going to visit **THE FOSSILS** after school that kept me going, because I KNEW they'd have something nice for me to eat. I'd even be happy to try one of Granny's ODD treats.

(Maybe not.)

BACK IN CLASS

The bell was just ABOUT to go for the end of the day when Mr Fullerman reminded us all that it was,

No school uniform day tomorrow.

Then he looked at me and said, **Don't forget, Tom!**

  "I <u>won't</u>, sir," I replied.

Marcus went and pulled THAT face again, which was annoying.

I left the class and told myself over and over again, "I will NOT forget no school uniform day – I will NOT forget no school uniform day."

I was on a mission to get to **THE FOSSILS'** house fast as I could hear my tummy rumbling.

Before I even rang the bell, Granddad opened the door wearing a very SNAZZY tank top.

He was very pleased to see me.

I told Granddad that I liked his **tank top** and he gave me a (very slow) twirl so I could see the back.

I guessed Granny Mavis must have made it – she L♡VES knitting. Granny can knit, talk and watch TV all at the same time. I think she's got some kind of

KNITTING **SUPER** POWER.

One minute she's holding a ball of wool.

The next she's knitted a brand new jumper and is WEARING IT, like *magic*.

I've tried studying WHAT her knitting needles are doing, but she moves her hands <u>SO</u> fast THAT EVERYTHING is a **BLUR.**

Once, I saw her use THREE needles all at the SAME TIME. Granny has serious knitting SKILLS. She is a knitting NINJA and Granddad is her **tank top** model – and doing a very good job, too! "Mavis is a WONDER with a ball of wool," Granddad said.

"This **tank top's** a bit special, isn't it, Tom?"
he added and smiled at me.

"It is, Granddad. Your tank top's the BEST,"
I agreed.

(Granddad looked a bit like a bumblebee with the
 stripes, but I didn't say
that because I could see
how much he loved it.)

Granny was sitting in her comfy chair and
already busy knitting something else.

"Is that another **tank top** for Granddad?"
I wondered.

"It's a scarf, Tom. I can show you how to
make your own if you want?"

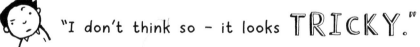
"I don't think so - it looks TRICKY."
But Granddad convinced me to have a go.

"Go on, Tom, even I've made a scarf.
Your granny's an excellent teacher."

Granny suddenly WHIPPED out two **GINORMOUS** knitting needles and a ball of very **FLUFFY** black wool. "These are what Bob used – his hands are a bit creaky, but you'll have no problem picking it up, Tom," Granny told me.

I wasn't so sure. The needles looked like drumsticks and I didn't know where to start. Granny helped me to get going, and I was concentrating so much I almost FORGOT how hungry I was. Knitting wasn't exactly what I'd been planning, but with Granny showing me what to do, after a while I began to see an

ACTUAL

SCARF

APPEARING ...

kind of.

 I was very slow, and happy when Granny took over and finished it off for me.

It was easy to spot the parts I'd knitted, but I was still pleased with my handiwork.

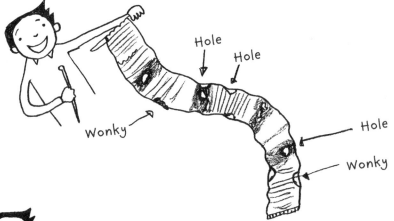

Hole

Hole

Wonky

Hole

Wonky

 I tried the scarf on and decided the messy bits of my knitting might even come in handy.

I would pretend my scarf was MEANT to look like that. Granny and Granddad thought I'd done a **GREAT** job!

"Well done, Tom. You must be hungry after all that concentrating?" Granddad asked.

"I AM!" I said, sounding slightly muffled from behind my scarf.

"Excellent. I've also knitted you a CAKE!" Granny told me, which was confusing, but also EXACTLY the sort of thing Granny would do.

"She's only joking, Tom." Granddad LAUGHED. He could see I was surprised.

Granny headed off to the kitchen.

"Though I'm sure Mavis COULD knit a cake if she wanted to," he added.

When Granny reappeared she offered me a plate of ... I don't know what. ?

After a **LONG** stare, I worked out they were made from:

chocolate sponge cake ✓

with lettuce topping, ✗

cherries ✓

and an unknown filling. ✗

Sometimes it's **BEST** not to know what's in Granny's cakes. I tried one anyway and told her it was delicious (keeping my favourite grandchild position, obviously). ☺

Thank you, Tom.

As my knitting had taken a while, Granddad offered to take me home. Thanks to his mobility scooter and super *SPEEDY* driving, we got back in no time at all.

Even with Granny Mavis ...

... hanging on to the back in rollerskates.

Weeeeeeee!

Mum and Dad were very impressed with my hand-knitted scarf. I even showed it to Delia. "I made it myself," I told her.

No... REALLY? I'd NEVER have guessed,

she laughed.

"I could make you one if you want?" I suggested.

"I like my scarves without holes, thanks. But it's Uncle Kevin's birthday soon – he'd LOVE a scarf, I'm sure."

Dad thought it was a good idea too. "For the man who has everything, a Tom Gates scarf would be perfect."

I really liked my scarf, and the holes were useful.

I was planning to show it to Derek tomorrow. He'd be impressed, I bet.

During the night, there was a BIG STORM
and lots of loud banging noises, which woke me up.
I was too tired to get up and see what it was.
I found out from Dad in the morning.
"Sorry about the noise last night, Tom.
All that rain. The shed roof was leaking a lot.
I had to run out and protect my computer and work."

"I thought you fixed the shed?"   I said.

 "So did I."

 (I didn't,) Mum added.

"I'm good at DIY normally,"
Dad protested.

"A bit like Tom's good at knitting?"
Delia joined in, which reminded me to
bring my scarf with me.

"h, Tom, your grandparents called early this morning," Mum said to me.

"They have something for you and want to meet you at the school gates. They seemed very EXCITED and wanted you to have it today."

 "Really?"

"It can only mean one thing, Tom. Granny's been cooking," said Delia, really enjoying herself.

I hoped she was wrong and it wasn't more layered chocolate sponge cakes with cherries and lettuce – I'd had enough of those.

I left the house a little later than normal and missed 𝔻erek, who'd already gone, so I'd have to show him my scarf at school.

When I arrived, THE FOSSILS were already waiting and waving from the school gates.

They seemed VERY pleased to see me.

"TOM, WE HAVE SOMETHING FOR YOU,"
Granddad said, and Granny handed over a gift bag.

Derek saw me and looked slightly confused.
"Is it for your birthday?"

"I don't think so, I just have lovely
grandparents," I told him.
(More favourite grandchild points for me. ✓)

I looked inside the bag and saw a neatly wrapped
present. It was very exciting.

My present was attracting a lot of attention from other kids, including AMY and Florence.

"Hey, Tom..." AMY began to say.
"No, it's not my birthday," I interrupted.

"Did you forget — it's no school uniform day,"
    Florence added.

   I FROZE mid-present-opening.

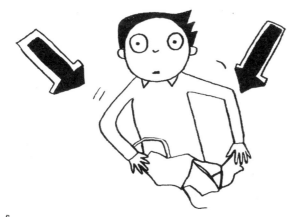

Looking around, I was the ONLY kid in school uniform.

HOW DID I FORGET IT WAS NO SCHOOL UNIFORM DAY?

I tried really hard not to let my disappointment SHOW on my face and carried on opening my present. And just when I thought things couldn't get worse...

"I **KNEW** you'd forget it was no school uniform day," I heard Marcus say.
He was wearing a very nice **DUDE 3** T-shirt too. (Like I should have been if I hadn't forgotten NO SCHOOL UNIFORM DAY.)

"This is perfect, Tom. I think you'll be pleased with your present – especially now," Granny and Granddad told me.

I opened it up and before I could say anything, Marcus shouted,

38

"Tank top!"

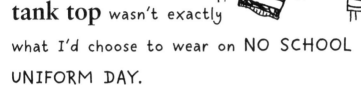

Don't get me wrong –
I <u>DID</u> like it, but a
tank top wasn't exactly
what I'd choose to wear on NO SCHOOL
UNIFORM DAY.
It was identical to Granddad's **tank top.**

Straight away, Granny began helping me to put it
on. I had no choice. As it went over my eyes, I
caught sight of Marcus smirking at me.

Granddad gave me the thumbs up and told me,
"Mavis knitted you your very own **tank top** all
because you liked mine SO much!"

With all my friends around me and **THE FOSSILS** looking so pleased, I couldn't say anything else BUT...

"Thanks, Granny. It's the ☆**BEST**☆ **STRIPEY tank top** I've ever had."

(Which was true as I've never had a **tank top** before.)

"It really does suit you," Florence said.

"And now you're OFFICIALLY part of no school uniform day!" **D**erek pointed out. I <u>was</u> pleased about that. :)

"We'd better be off, Tom. We can't miss the start of our **HOT YOGA** class," Granny announced while Granddad demonstrated a few FLEXING MOVES.

"Bob! Don't peak too soon! Save some energy for the class," Granny told him before they waved goodbye.

Derek noticed he had on the same T-shirt as Marcus as we headed into school.

"Look, we're matching! DUDE 3 are the best band!" Derek told him.

"I like the T-shirt better than the band," Marcus said. "And I KNEW you'd forget it was no school uniform day, Tom," he added smugly.

"Well, at least I'll be the only person in the entire school wearing a stripey **tank top,**" I said, trying to pretend it was a good thing. "Sometimes, Marcus, forgetting things can work out for the best," I told him.

(Or that's what I thought...)

How was I supposed to know that Mr Fullerman had a stripey **tank top** as well?

Brilliant.

(Not in a good way.)

(Oh well, at least no one has a scarf like mine, so I wasn't dressed EXACTLY the same as Mr Fullerman after all.)

2

Tasty Treats

Mum said she was going to drop me off at school this morning.

 "Are we driving?" I asked, because I like it when I get an unexpected LIFT in the car. 😊

"No, I've got a dentist appointment, so I'm not going to work until later. I thought I could walk with you and Derek for a change,"
Mum told me, then added,

"OH, and THAT reminds me."

 It's NEVER a good sign when my parents say that.

For instance ➡

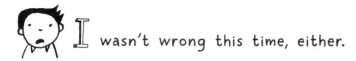 I wasn't wrong this time, either.

"I **MUST** book you in to see the dentist as well. It's been far too long," Mum said.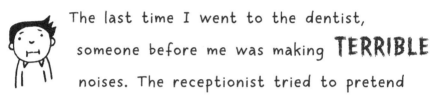

I could see Mum was LOOKING at my teeth, so I closed my mouth fast.

The last time I went to the dentist, someone before me was making **TERRIBLE** noises. The receptionist tried to pretend like NOTHING was happening and gave me some stickers so I had something to do.

I coloured them in while I was waiting, but it didn't help much. I kept thinking about bad teeth.

OH! AGhh! Owww... Oooo... AGhhhh! OOOOwwww... Awwwww...

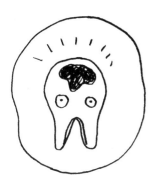

Mum told me not to worry.

"THOSE are the sounds of someone who hasn't been for a check-up in a very LONG TIME, Tom. THAT'S why you have to brush your teeth, not eat too many sweets and go to the dentist regularly," she explained.

If she was trying to make me feel better, it didn't work. I reminded her about those "AGH" noises and how my appointment had to be cancelled because the dentist was too busy with whoever was in there.

"EXACTLY, Tom. You can't leave it so long to see the dentist."

(That wasn't what I wanted to hear.)

Derek was waiting for me outside his house.
He SMILED when he saw me, then stopped
when he spotted Mum.
(It was a bit OBVIOUS.)

"Morning, Derek - I'm joining you for
your walk to school!" said Mum cheerfully.

"Morning, Mrs Gates - the **WHOLE** way
to school?" asked Derek.

"That's right! All the way!"

Something was up with Derek - I could tell.
He whispered to me. "I've found some change
and I wanted to stop at the shop to buy a treat!"
Now Mum was with us, she wouldn't let us stop
to buy treats before school, that's for sure.
Derek and I just had to LOOK at it and walk
past really S L O W L Y.

WAFERS

"We'll do it on the way home," I assured Derek.

"Do what, Tom?" Mum asked, because she always hears EVERYTHING.

"Homework, Mum..." I said quickly.

Mum smiled and took out a piece of paper. I thought it was my REAL homework and PANICKED.

"What's that?" I asked.

"It's a letter from school..." Mum told me.

"Oh no."

"About all the new events the parents and carers association are putting on, including a sponsored silence!" Mum read out to us.

"You'll get a lot of sponsors for that."

Mum LAUGHED.

  "My mum's being funny," I told Derek.

When we got to school, there was a VERY interesting stall set up in the school grounds with LOTS of nice-looking things on it.

"Hey, Tom – can you see what I can see?" Derek asked me.

"I think I can."

It was a  of mini wafers.

We weren't the only kids to spot it.

While Mum was chatting to another parent, we rushed over for a closer look.

"HOW do you win THAT?" I wanted to know.

"You buy a raffle ticket. They're a pound each, and **ALL** the money goes to the school," one of the dads running the stall told us.

"Do the teachers use it for treats?" Derek asked.

"No – it's for the SCHOOL, for equipment," the dad said, but no one was really listening. We were all focused on the WAFERS.

"How do you win THAT?" Leroy wanted
to know, pointing at the tin.

"Like I said, with a raffle ticket. A letter
went out last week telling everyone all about it.
Does anyone want to buy one?" the dad asked.

"Can't you JUST win the wafers?"  another kid said.

"No, it's the LUCK of the draw. But all the
prizes are FANTASTIC!"
said the dad, trying to convince us.

I wasn't so SURE because some things
looked a lot better than others.
In my head I picked the prizes I wouldn't mind
winning. The wafer tin FIRST (obviously).

Chocolate World voucher

YES - I'd like that
☺

Not a bad
thing to win

BOX of
GAMES

YES PLEASE!

PENS and paper

Treat hamper NICE!

What's this?

TEACHER TEA

CAKES YES!

TREAT

Squash ← Not so much

Apart from odd tin of strange paste

There were some cupcakes with a sign saying "Teacher Tea Treat". I liked the cakes but wasn't sure about the <u>teacher</u> bit. Kids were still asking about the wafers when Mum came to join us.

"Would you like to buy a raffle ticket ?" the dad wanted to know, sounding a little more desperate.

"Yes, why not? One for you, Tom, and one each for $\mathbb{D}$erek and ME!" Mum told him and handed over the money.

The dad tore off the tickets and told Mum, "It's all for a good cause!"

"Yes the teachers are all having a big PARTY!" I said as a $\mathbb{JOKE}$.

HOW WAS I SUPPOSED TO KNOW MR FULLERMAN WAS STANDING RIGHT BEHIND ME?

"I can ASSURE you the money's all going to fund school equipment, Tom. Though a party does sound like a good idea!"

Mr Fullerman said.

(It was awkward.)

"Listen out for Mrs Mumble's announcement of the RAFFLE winners at the end of the day," the stall holder told us.

Derek and I were getting excited about the wafer tin when Mum decided to remind me about the DENTIST.

"Those wafers wouldn't be great for your TEETH, Tom. Especially if you're going to the dentist," she told me, then hugged me goodbye.

Mr Fullerman tried to move everyone away from the stall. Though some kids were still asking QUESTIONS.

> How do you win the wafers?

> Can I have a wafer?

> Can I get a ticket for the wafers?

(I think the dad on the stall was pleased to see us go.)

Derek and I put our tickets safely in our bags and crossed our fingers that WE would <u>win</u> that tin.

I sat down next to **AMY** in class and she handed me something under the desk and said, "Tom, here – don't let **Mr Fullerman** see." I looked down and in her hand was a fruit chew.

(It was a GOOD start to the day.) ☺

 "Save it for later, OK?" she suggested.

I took the chew quickly and said, "Thanks!"

"WHAT have you got there?" Marcus asked me, being nosy.

Mr Fullerman was already STANDING in front of the class, so I said, "Nothing."

I thought about eating the chew and decided to wait for the right moment.

"Hello, Class 5F. Anyone who's taken part in the RAFFLE – good luck. Someone is in for a REAL TREAT! They won't be disappointed."

Now seemed like a good time to unwrap my chew. Doing it quietly was going to be a challenge. Marcus was already looking.

RUSTLE
RUSTLE

I expertly tore off the paper, then did the "I'm YAWNING" hand move to pop the **fruit chew** in my mouth. It was a **BOLD** step.

YAWN

It wasn't easy to do with a sticky **fruit chew**. I was already beginning to regret trying it, but I had to finish it now.

Every time Mr Fullerman turned his back to write something on the board, I did some EXTRA FAST CHEWING to try and finish it quickly.

"Are you eating?"

Marcus whispered to me. I ignored him and kept chewing and THAT'S when it happened.

Crunch AWWW

I felt something in my mouth go crunch, and accidentally let out an "AWWWWW!" sound.

 Mr Fullerman turned round immediately and gave me a look.

"No eating in class, Tom. Put it in the bin now please. You know the RULES."

"BIG mistake," Marcus muttered.

AMY rolled her eyes at me.

"You were supposed to SAVE it!" she whispered.

I put what was left of my chew in my hand, and that's when I saw it...

 A filling had come out of my tooth. It didn't FEEL very good either.

"SIR, my filling fell out," I told him.

Mr Fullerman shook his head.
"Oh dear, Tom, sweets in class are not a good idea. Does it hurt?"

 "No... YES, it does a bit."

My tooth HAD begun to throb a little. I put my chew and filling in the bin and sat down. But for the rest of the class, I couldn't concentrate.

My tooth began to REALLY ache.

Mr Fullerman saw I was in pain and sent me to the school office to see Mrs Mumble, who would call Mum.

 (I wished I hadn't had that chew.)

AMY said she was sorry she gave it to me. But it wasn't her fault.

"Bad luck, Tom," Marcus told me. "No more sweets for you," he added, when there was no need to.

I was waiting outside the school office feeling sorry for myself when I noticed I could see into the TEACHERS' STAFF ROOM.

The place NO CHILDREN were ALLOWED.
I spotted comfy chairs, a big table and the adults who were ... SMILING. I had been in there before but it looked different.

STAFF ROOM
↑
KNOCK PLEASE

Mrs Mumble stood in front of me, blocking my view of the staff room. She came to tell me that Mum would be picking me up VERY soon.

"Luckily for you, Tom, she's at the dentist's right now and they've agreed to see you for an EMERGENCY appointment. That's good news, isn't it?"
Mrs Mumble said.

I nodded slowly at the thrilling news.

All I had to do now was work out EXACTLY what I would say to Mum. It was probably best to SKIP the **fruit chew** bit.

I tried to focus on the REALLY good news that I'd be leaving school early (even if it was just to go to the dentist).

 As soon as Mum arrived, she wanted to know what had happened. "You were fine this morning. Were you eating something?" she asked, just as I pointed to my missing filling so I didn't have to answer.

Mum sighed. "OK, we'd better get going."

"It just sort of FELL OUT," I whispered. Which it sort of did. Mum had the car, so we got to the dentist's in double quick time. When I opened my mouth to show the dentist my teeth, a bit of my **fruit chew** made an unwelcome appearance.

"Oh ... this might have something to do with the filling falling out," the dentist said.

$\mathbb{I}$ shrugged my shoulders in a "HOW DID THAT GET THERE?" kind of way, like it was a **fruit chew** mystery. fruit chew – ?

My dentist was very nice and nothing hurt at all. I got the "Brush your teeth and don't eat sweets" talk and I was given the choice of picking

my own sticker. →

SMILE

I was looking forward to going back home for a nice restful time as my appointment was over so fast.

But Mum had other ideas.

"Don't be silly, Tom. It's only a new filling. You don't want to MISS a whole day of school too, do you?"

(I did.)

Mum got me back to class in time for the extra spelling test...

... which was a lot more painful than losing a filling.

 **"Nice to see you're OK, Tom, and GREAT NEWS you won't miss the test,"** Mr Fullerman told me and smiled. I found it HARD to share his enthusiasm, ←—but I did the best I could in the test.

My face was still a bit NUMB from the dentist's and I found myself poking it without thinking.

"Should you be doing that?" AMY wondered.

"Probably not," I agreed and tried to stop.

"Tom, you're doing it again," **AMY** said, so I stopped pressing my cheek as the feeling was coming back to me slowly.

"AND you shouldn't eat SWEETS in class, or anywhere, if you have a new filling," Marcus enjoyed reminding me.

"Thanks for that, Marcus – that's what my dentist said too," I sighed.

"So if you win the big jar of wafers in the raffle, you should give them to me. I'll be HELPING to save your teeth," Marcus said happily.

I'D FORGOTTEN ABOUT THE RAFFLE!

The chances of me winning the **GIANT TIN** of wafers were small — I knew that — but it didn't stop me  **THINKING**

about wafers for the rest of the school day and right up until home time.

Before the bell went, Mrs Mumble CRACKLED over the tannoy to make the raffle ANNOUNCEMENT.

"Quiet, everyone,"
Mr Fullerman said so we could listen to the raffle numbers being drawn. The whole class was silent. You could have heard a WAFER drop.

Number 14... Number 21... Number 16...
(Not mine) Number 2... 10... 18... 29... 50...

It wasn't hard to spot who'd won something in our class.

Norman made so much noise
that we missed the next number.

"... is the LAST number, thank you, everyone."

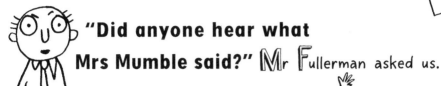**"Did anyone hear what Mrs Mumble said?"** Mr Fullerman asked us.

Indrani put up her hand.

   "I think she said 57, sir."

Then **AMY** nudged me and pointed at my ticket.

"You're 57, Tom."

"Remember, I'll help you eat any wafers," Marcus added. I was STUNNED. I'd never won anything **THIS** important before. I ran over and celebrated with Norman. Mr Fullerman suggested we both **"CALM DOWN"** then told us to **"Go to the office to find out what you've won."**

   We didn't need reminding about THAT!

57

Is my NEW FAVOURITE number. 😊

The first thing I did was find Derek, who was

almost as EXCITED as ME.

YES YES YES Tom! YES

Clutching my ticket tightly, we

both rushed down to the school office and joined

the WINNERS' queue. The little kids were at the

front (as usual) when Mrs Mumble called us in one

by one to get our PRIZES.

Derek and I crossed our fingers and hoped that no one would come out holding the wafer tin.

"Phew ... looks like the squash has gone," Derek whispered as a kid appeared holding it.

Then Norman came out looking EXCITED.

"So many nice things in this hamper – apart from this weird PASTE,"

he told us, then shouted, "I LOVE RAFFLES!"

We did too, until a girl walked past smiling and said, "My life is complete!"

The tin of wafers was GONE.

Derek and I were GUTTED.

"There must be other great things to win," Derek tried to reassure me. We didn't have long to wait until Mrs Mumble called us in.

What **HAD** we won?

There was only one thing left propped up on her desk.

"Tom – ticket number 57 – you are very lucky to get this treat. I can assure you THIS is something that MONEY can't buy," Mrs Mumble was pleased to tell us.

 "Like another MASSIVE tin of wafers?" Derek wondered.

"Even better than that..."

"Tickets to a DUDE3 concert!" I shouted.

"No, Tom – but you won't be disappointed."

I gave Mrs Mumble my raffle ticket and picked up the card.

"It's tickets to *Chocolate World!* YES!"

 I said excitedly.

"Not exactly, Tom. But you'll have a  **FANTASTIC** time, I promise.

It's a treat for two, so you could bring Derek," Mrs Mumble told us both.

"I can't wait!" I said excitedly. "You'll come, won't you, Derek?"

"Try and STOP me!" he said and then we read the card.

"Can I change my mind?" Derek asked me.

"Don't you dare."

It wasn't exactly the treat we were hoping for.

One Week Later

"Right, are you ready, Derek? Still hungry?"
I asked before we went in.

"I am," Derek said.

(That's why he's my best friend.)

Having tea with the teachers wasn't exactly *Chocolate World*, but THAT'S what I'd won in the raffle.

On the PLUS SIDE, Derek and I actually got to see INSIDE the staff room, which NEVER happens.

 We'd be able to tell all our friends what it was REALLY like. And the teachers did put on the most fantastic-looking spread of food for the special TEA.

Mrs Worthington was there, Mrs Nap, Mr Fullerman, and even Mr Keen came to join us.

"How's your band Bobzombies doing, boys?" he asked.

"DOGZOMBIES, sir," Derek corrected him.

"Exactly. Well, I hope you both enjoy this lovely tea!"

Mr Keen told us, not really listening.

(We did our best.)

78

When Mrs Worthington gave out the caramel
wafers, things really picked up. It seemed like a good
time to show the teachers how to do the caramel
wafer trick.

"You have to guess which is the empty wafer,"
        I explained.

It had them all guessing – apart from Derek...

... who knew EXACTLY which wafer was EMPTY*.

Unlike the teachers, who all got it wrong.

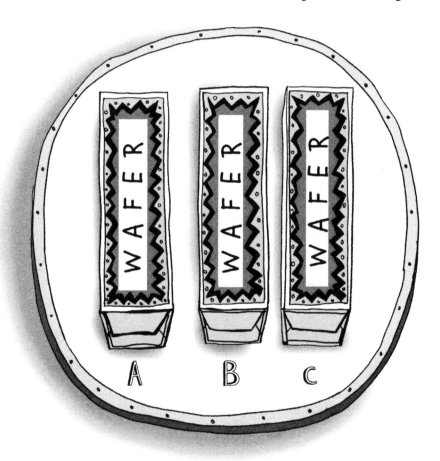

*Answer on page 238

Can <u>you</u> spot the
empty wafer?

I'll give you THREE guesses who Mum and Dad have asked to look after me this afternoon.

1. THE FOSSILS? (No, they're busy.)

2. Derek's Mum and Dad? (No, Derek's out for the day.)

3. Delia?

(YES — that's right, my cheerful sister.) You can tell from her face that she's THRILLED about it. (I'm not exactly pleased, either.)

Here's what happened.

I was having a relaxing day doodling in my notebook, reading comics, and doing nice things when Mum and Dad announced they were going out to a DIY shop.

Huh?

In case you don't know what **DIY** stands for, it's Do It Yourself. (Or it could be ...
Dogs in Yellow - I wouldn't mind going to that shop.)

YELLOW
YELLOW

Mum told Delia, "We're leaving you in charge for an hour or so while we go out."

It's the "or so" bit that usually means they're going to be AGES.
Straight away, Delia wasn't happy.

"I can't do it. I'm going out too. I'm not looking after Tom," she snapped.

I could tell she was only going to get WORSE.
The thought of Delia being in charge for a few hours wasn't GREAT.

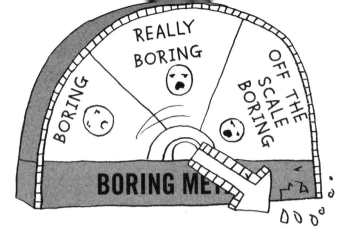

"Exactly HOW long are you going to be?"
I asked Mum.

"We need to get a new floor for your dad's shed
after the roof leaked and ruined it.
And a few other things too."

THAT was a WARNING for me –
"A FEW OTHER THINGS". Mum and Dad would
be going to HUNDREDS of other shops as well.

Dad told me I could come along if I wanted to.

"But you can't drag your feet all day, Tom –
we need to get going."

I had a BIG decision to make.

(1) Go with Mum and Dad and be VERY bored.

(2) Stay at home with Delia who was VERY grumpy and also in charge (so NO snacks).

 "We'll be much quicker if you BOTH stay here. It will be nice to spend some quality time together," Mum told us. Delia and I weren't so sure about that.

"I'm NOT babysitting Tom all afternoon," Delia said to Mum and Dad before they left

 (like I was spoiling her *FUN*).

But that got me thinking...

"**W**hy is it called babysitting? It's not like you **SIT** on me and I'm not a baby."

"I don't know, Tom. Haven't you got something better to do?" Delia wanted to know.

 "Not really."

"Can you stop following me around?" Delia sighed, which made me want to do it more.

 "I've got an idea - I could show you how to draw a ... **MONSTER!**" I suggested.

"No, Tom. What I REALLY want to do is go to the shopping centre book store.

But I can't, thanks to you."

"It's not MY FAULT,"

I reminded Delia, who unexpectedly said,
"OK, Tom - how about we play a game instead?"

 "What game?"

"Hide and seek. You go and hide
and I'll come and look for you."

I wasn't going to fall for THAT old trick -
where Delia doesn't bother trying to find me at ALL.
But I pretended to think about it anyway.

"Hmmm... OK, but I'll need a SNACK FIRST."

(It was worth a try.)

"NO snacks," Delia snapped, then
added, "Look, Tom - IF you come with me
to the shopping centre, I'll make it worth your while."

"But I don't want to go to the shopping centre.
I don't want to go shopping, and I'm not changing
my mind," I told Delia firmly.

It was Delia's SUDDEN mention of buying me
TREATS that really helped me to think again.

Right now, I'm enjoying delicious caramel popcorn
and a slushy drink that <u>will</u> turn my mouth blue.
(I'm not normally allowed them, so it was the
FIRST thing I asked for.)

Big bag

I've brought a bag with all my essential stuff to keep me busy, just in case Delia takes **AGES** in the book store.

"Did you HAVE to bring that big bag, Tom?"

"EVERYTHING in here is useful!" I explain.

"I doubt it. Come on, hurry up. We need to get to the top floor," Delia says, and makes me run after her.

I'm trying not to spill my popcorn or drink as we get on the escalator. Looking up, I can SEE loads of people queuing at the book store already, which makes me pleased I brought my bag.

"I'm SO LATE – this is annoying," Delia mutters.

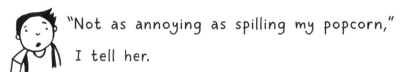

"Not as annoying as spilling my popcorn," I tell her.

(Delia ignores me.)

We have to join
the queue RIGHT at the BACK,
which is a long way from the book store.
I'm not exactly happy about it, but Delia's FURIOUS.

"Why are we HERE again?"
I ask her, not helping the situation.

"I'm going to get my favourite author's <u>latest</u>
book signed. She's amazing!" Delia sounds *ALMOST*
ENTHUSIASTIC.

"It's like if I met , then?"

SLURP

"Sort of," Delia agrees.

We move one place down the queue as I
finish my drink. "What's the book about?"

"Why do you ask so many questions, Tom?"
Delia grumbles, then says...

"The book's all about being POSITIVE ...
and STOP slurping your drink!"

"That's not very positive..." I whisper.
We shuffle forwards a bit more. I begin to realize
that I might need the toilet. Just thinking about
it makes it WORSE. I know Delia will be annoyed.

"STOP jiggling around!"
she tells me.

"I can't help it - I need the toilet."

"YOU'RE KIDDING!"
Delia is almost shouting.

A nice person in front of us points out that the
toilets are closed. "You'll have to go to the ground
floor - I'll keep your place." Which is kind of them.

Delia says, "Thank you," then grumpily takes me
back down.

"Sorry, it's the slushy," I explain, which doesn't help.

I finish my drink and hand my popcorn bag and empty cup to Delia.

"Just HuRRY uP, TOM!"

she says, getting annoyed.

"DON'T eat any of my popcorn, will you?"
I tell her in case she gets any ideas.

It's a **BIG** relief when I come out of the toilet. Delia hands me back my stuff, and I CHECK my popcorn level.

"I haven't TOUCHED it - can we go?"
she snaps at me.

"OK, let's take the lift," I suggest, trying to be helpful - but Delia doesn't seem that keen.

"That's a GLASS lift, Tom. I hate heights!"

"Really?" I ask as that's NEWS to me.

"I'm just trying to be helpful,"

I add.

Reluctantly, Delia agrees.

"FINE!" She follows me into the lift and the door closes. I press a few buttons as we're the only people inside.

"HuRRY uP, TOM!" Delia tells me.

(She sounds TENSE.)

We start to move and Delia CLUTCHES the handrail **VERY** tightly.

"L**OO**K how high up we are!" I point out.

Delia keeps quiet. I walk round to see the view.

"DON'T MOVE, TOM. I don't like it!" Delia tells me.

"Nearly at the TOP!" I let her know cheerily, when the lift suddenly **STOPS.**

"**What** have you done?" Delia shouts.

"Nothing! I haven't touched a thing!"

I press the fourth floor button a few more times.

"Why aren't we MOVING?" she asks.

"I think we're stuck," I say helpfully.

"This <u>can't</u> be happening!"
Delia sounds **CROSS.**

I try the **EMERGENCY** button and we hear a voice that asks us what's happened.

"The lift's stuck," I say.

"We'll have an engineer out to you as quickly as we can," they tell us calmly.

"HOW QUICKLY?" Delia wants to know.

"VERY SOON – you'll be OUT in no time at all," the voice crackles.

"I'm here with my brother, who's only little," Delia adds for some reason.

"HEY! I'm not that little, and YOU'RE the one who doesn't like heights," I remind her.

The voice disappears and Delia and I glare at each other for a while. She's cross that we got in the lift. I'm fed up too. I could be at home watching TV. The only good news is that I have my emergency bag with me, which is going to come in handy.

I can hear Delia talking to herself quietly – like I'm not even here!

"Why did I listen to Tom?" she's saying.

"It's not MY fault. You don't normally listen to me," I tell her and take a big handful of popcorn.

"Aren't you going to give me any popcorn then?" she asks.

 "I wasn't planning on it – there's not much left."

"I'll remember THAT," Delia says in a sort of threatening kind of way. So, reluctantly, I pass it over and INSTANTLY regret it.

"Thanks, Tom."

"You took LOADS!"

(I don't give her any more.)

Half an hour later

All my popcorn's gone and we're still

STUCK. We can hear the engineer outside

trying to fix the lift. They shout down,

"Are you two OK? We won't be long."

"Oh yes – we're having the BEST time,"

Delia calls back. (I'm not sure she means it.)

This feels like a good time to look in my bag.

"What have you got in there?" she asks me.

"Useful things – like THIS!"

I pull out a small cushion that I took from

our sofa. "I thought this might come

in handy and I was RIGHT,"

I say and sit down on it. "Comfy!"

"A cushion?" she repeats.

"And ... my lucky monster pebble! See?"

Delia sighs. "It's not *THAT* lucky, is it?"

"I'm never going to get my book signed now."

(She looks really fed up.)

 "I'm just glad I went to the toilet,"
I add, then try to cheer Delia up by saying,

"The book queue was MASSIVE, Delia.
You might still get there in time."

"I doubt it..."

I point to her book.
"Positive thinking - that's what your book says."

"Have you got anything else in your bag to eat?"
Delia asks me. I have another RUMMAGE and bring
out a FEAST.

An open packet of cheese crackers and
half a caramel wafer.

"It was all I could grab before we left," I explain.

"I wasn't planning on sharing it, but I will."

(I am being NICE.)

"Go on, then..."

Delia tells me as I divide the snacks up almost equally. (They are mine after all.)

 "Thanks, Tom. This could be a Granny Mavis snack."

"It's better than vegetable cake or carrots and custard," I tell her.

"Once, Granny gave me pasta with banana and spinach sauce."

(I was shocked by that.)

I take out my sticky notes,  pens and notepad from my bag and put them on the floor.

 "Do you want to play a game while we're waiting?" I ask Delia.

"No, Tom, I don't want to play a game. I want to get out of this LIFT." She sounds SNAPPY.

"Am I an animal?"

"Yes."

"Am I **FURRY?**"

"Yes."

"Am I a dog?"

"No." My turn.

"Am <u>I</u> an animal?"

"Yes."

"Am <u>I</u> **FURRY?**"

"Yes."

"Do I have a TAIL?"

"Yes."

"Do I smell?"

"Yes."

"Am I a skunk?"

"Did you cheat?"

(A little bit – I could see my reflection in the glass, but I don't tell Delia that.)

"No. I'm not playing another game, Tom,"

she tells me. "I'm too FED UP..."

(102)

The engineer SHOUTS down to us once more,

"NEARLY THERE! NOT LONG NOW."

"PLEASE HURRY UP!" Delia shouts back.
More people are staring up at us as we've been
stuck in here for ages. I have an idea and do some
doodling on my notepad.

"What are you doing NOW?"

Delia wants to know.

"Something you'll be pleased about," I tell her.

"I doubt that," she says.
I write out a message and hold it up so the crowd
can see. I can tell people are reading it.
"People like my sign, Delia. It's going to be OK," I say.

"That's great, Tom," Delia adds wearily.

She's not interested at all.

Ten minutes later, the lift SHUDDERS
and we start to slowly MOVE UP.

It's a BIG RELIEF!

The manager and engineer are HAPPY to see us
– but not as HAPPY as we are. :)
The BAD news is: the author has already finished
the signing and the books have all gone.

Surprisingly, Delia doesn't seem too bothered.
"I'm desperate for the toilet," she says.

"The nearest one's on the ground floor.

You could take the lift,"

the manager reminds us.

"Are you kidding?" Delia says,

and we take the ESCALATOR back down.

While Delia's gone, the manager
hands me a bag.
"I saw your sign and meant to give you THIS.
It's the LEAST we could do to apologize for the lift
breaking down. Now, is there anything else I can get you?"
I take a look in the bag, and see what it is.

"YES, thank you – there is something I'd like,"
I say quickly before Delia comes back.

MORE POPCORN !

And this time, I make sure Delia gets her own.

 We've been gone for nearly THREE hours, but we still get home before Mum and Dad. It's obvious from all the STUFF they've bought that they went to a LOT more than one shop. I'm actually glad I went with Delia.

Mum says we can go to the shopping centre NOW and Delia SNAPS...

"There's no need - we've MISSED everything. All the books will have gone."

(She doesn't mention the lift.)

This seems like a very good time to step in and hand over the bag that the manager gave me.

But FIRST I try and get Delia to say...
"Repeat after me – Tom is the **BEST**
brother ever. I will be nice to him all the time."

Delia looks confused. "WHY would I say that?"

Then she sees what's in the bag – only the book she wanted to buy!

It's a strange experience watching Delia be pleased about something.

Almost a smile --->

And thanks to my SIGN, the manager got the author to sign it too.

Delia is forced to agree that I am the best brother ever.

My sister Delia wants a book signed – but we're STUCK in the LIFT!

Mum wants to know how we got the book. Then she asks if I've done my homework, which is awkward.

"It's a long story," Delia says and doesn't mention the popcorn, blue slushy, or getting stuck in the lift at all. (Best not to.)

I've put Delia in such a good mood, she EVEN offers to help me with my homework, which I say YES to

(obviously).

I try and make the most of this situation while she's so happy and ask if I can borrow a few of her **ROCK WEEKLY** magazines.

"And I wouldn't mind a wafer as well?"

I ask hopefully.

"Don't push it, Tom," Delia says.

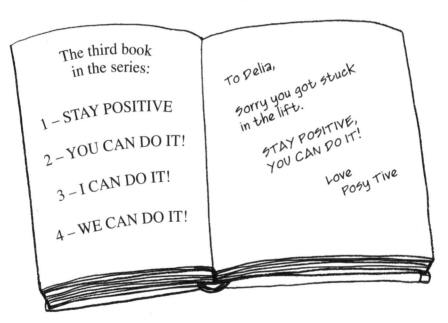

The third book
in the series:

1 – STAY POSITIVE

2 – YOU CAN DO IT!

3 – I CAN DO IT!

4 – WE CAN DO IT!

To Delia,

Sorry you got stuck
in the lift.

STAY POSITIVE,
YOU CAN DO IT!

Love
Posy Tive

(It was worth a go. It's not often I'm in Delia's good books.)

FOUR TREMENDOUS TAILS

But what animals do they belong to?

Answers on page 238

Practising for my sponsored silence ...

... is not easy, thanks to the fly.

Our headmaster Mr Keen made an ANNOUNCEMENT in assembly. He said...

"This year for the first time EVER, we'll be taking part in the Oakfield Town ... Children's Parade!"

Then he did an *AIR PUNCH*, which was unexpected.

"LET'S show everyone how AMAZING our school is!"

he told us and waited for a big `CHEER`.

No one was sure what to do, apart from Brad Galloway who shouted, "YEAH!"

and someone else coughed really loudly.

"Emails are being sent to your homes which explain all about it," Mr Keen added.

I was pretty excited about the parade, but when Mum and Dad got the email they didn't seem that excited at ALL.

"Oh no ... more costumes," Mum sighed.

"Aren't we busy that weekend? I'm sure we're doing something," Dad asked.

Even Delia joined in with the grumbling about it.

"Just what Oakfield needs – a parade closing the WHOLE TOWN down."

Mr Fullerman says we'll have a school float and there's a recycled instrument SAMBA BAND too," I told them, thinking it made the parade sound even BETTER.

"Another good reason to miss it," Delia told me before disappearing to her room.

"Well, I'm still going," I said to Mum and Dad.

BACK IN CLASS

Mr Fullerman began to tell us more about the parade.

"You'll be asked to wear either RED, YELLOW OR GREEN clothing to fit in with OUR THEME this year, which is..."

... traffic lights.

I whisper, and AMY LAUGHS.

"The NATURAL WORLD," Mr Fullerman finishes saying and gives me a LOOK. **"I need ONE person to wear the MAIN costume and sit ON the float while the rest of you will walk in the parade."**

(I like the idea of sitting on the main float – I WANT to be THAT person.) Then Brad Galloway suddenly SHOUTS out...

"SIR, can I sit on the FLOAT?"
and the whole class joins in.

"ME! SIR!"

"CAN I SIT ON THE FLOAT, SIR!"

"I'LL DO IT, SIR!"

"ME! SIR!"

"Calm down, Class 5F. I'll be choosing <u>that</u> person in a fair way," he tells us.

Mr Fullerman points to the MERIT BOARD.
"The TOP five children on the merit board will have the chance to be on the FLOAT."

We <u>all</u> look at the board.

AMY'S name is there, as well as Indrani, Trevor, Marcus and ME. YES!
Before I get too excited, AMY spots a problem.

"Mr Fullerman, we've all got the same amount of MERITS."

"You're RIGHT, Amy. I'm going to have to decide based on who impresses me with their good behaviour!" Mr Fullerman tells us.

(This children's parade is SUDDENLY sounding like a MISSION to me.)

STRAIGHT AWAY Marcus tries to be helpful and offers to hand out today's worksheets.

Mr Fullerman, I'll help.

"Thank you, Marcus."

"And I'll push the chairs in at breaktime,"
Indrani tells **Mr Fullerman** quickly.

(I need to catch up and do something!)

 Even **AMY** is sorting out pencils.

I'm SO ready to help out and impress when
Mr Fullerman asks us a question.

I LISTEN really carefully.

**"Can I have a VOLUNTEER to take this
envelope down to the school office, please?"**

YES!

THIS IS MY CHANCE

I *LEAP* UP excitedly and accidentally WAVE my hand in Trevor Peters' face.

He drops all the pencils on the floor.

"Oh... Sorry, Trevor!" I apologize, and bend down to pick them up. This gives Marcus the opportunity to ═══*SWOOP* in and tell Mr Fullerman that he can take the envelope.

"I'll do it, SIR!"═══

"Don't be long, Marcus – thank you," Mr Fullerman tells him.

"Do I get another merit for helping, sir?" Marcus asks.

(THIS is getting ANNOYING.)

"Actually, Marcus, I've decided that we'll draw STRAWS to see who goes on the main float," Mr Fullerman says.

But Marcus has gone already.

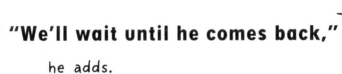

"We'll wait until he comes back," he adds.

So it's Trevor, **AMY,** Me and Indrani who'll draw straws.

... and Marcus.

Mr Fullerman is holding the five straws in his hand. You can't see the end of any of them. We don't know which straw is the short one. Whoever picks it will get to go on the float and wear the MAIN costume.

The atmosphere in the classroom is

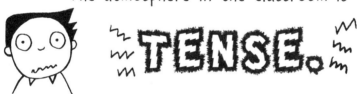

TENSE.

Marcus makes it worse by running in and shouting,

"I'M HERE!"

as if we'd missed him.

"Don't forget, children, you'll still be playing a very important part in the parade if you don't pick the short straw," Mr Fullerman reminds us.

We all reach for a straw and Trevor takes the first one out. I can tell from his face it's a long straw. It's AMY next, then Indrani, and then me. And we've all got ...

long straws.

Marcus has got the SHORT straw.

He's going to be the one on the FLOAT wearing the main costume.

For the rest of the day, Marcus doesn't stop going **on** about it.

"HANDS UP if you're sitting on the main float in the OAKFIELD SCHOOL PARADE?

JUST ME, THEN!"

Sigh

I'll be glad when the day of the parade actually arrives.

I've always loved short straws. Bad luck, Tom.

And when it finally does, I get to wear a red T-shirt with spots like Derek. Everyone else is dressed as insects in green or yellow.

Everyone apart from Marcus.

Thanks to the short straw, he's sitting up on the main float ...

... dressed as an apple.

I'm glad I didn't draw the short straw after all.

(Marcus did enjoy himself ... eventually.)

6

Silly Games

Recycled Plastic Cup

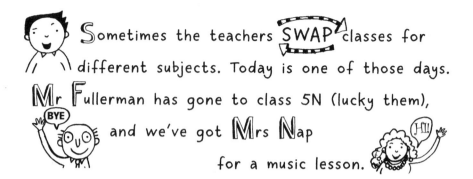

Sometimes the teachers SWAP classes for different subjects. Today is one of those days. Mr Fullerman has gone to class 5N (lucky them), and we've got Mrs Nap for a music lesson.

Let me tell you a few things about Mrs Nap.

* She is **VERY** enthusiastic all of the time.

* She can SING REALLY LOUDLY.

* She wears a LOT of chunky jewellery that makes CLONKING noises when she moves around.

(Like this) Clonk Clonk Clonk

Mrs Nap brings in a BIG box of what looks like kitchen equipment, which is unexpected. She holds up two wooden spoons and asks,

"Can anyone guess what we'll be doing with THESE today?"

(138)

"COOKING?"

Brad Galloway calls out from the back of the class. There's a rumble of excitement at the thought of doing something different.

"Can we make CAKES?" Amber Tully Green wants to know.

"Not today – anyone else want to have a guess?" Mrs Nap says and picks up a CHEESE grater next. Norman starts waving frantically.

"IT'S a CHEESE GRATER!" he shouts.

"Yes, Norman, but what are we going to do with it?" Mrs Nap asks.

"GRATE CHEESE?" Norman replies.
"I really like cheese, Mrs Nap," he adds.

"I like cheese too, Mrs Nap," Pansy tells her.

"I prefer cheese triangles," Solid adds.

There's a BIG discussion about cheese around the class, which wasn't the music lesson Mrs Nap was hoping for.

"This is RIDICULOUS," Marcus mumbles next to me. He's been saying "RIDICULOUS!" a lot lately, like it's his new favourite word.

AMY puts up her hand and asks Mrs Nap,

"Are we going to use the cheese grater like an instrument?"

"Well done, Amy, that's EXACTLY what we're going to do.

Before we begin, let's do some DEEP breathing exercises. Everyone stand up and TRY not to SCRAPE..."

SCRAPE SCRAPE

SCRAPE

she adds, just a little too late.
"NOW BREATHE in through your mouth and OUT through your nose,"

she tells us. (This confuses me.)

I'm not the only one either. There's a lot of BREATHING noises around the class.
Marcus sounds like a deflating balloon, he's breathing SO heavily.

PUFF

"Hey, Marcus, you're making my hair PUFF up,"
I tell him (he ignores me).

"You should ALL be feeling nice and relaxed now."

(Not really.)

Then Mrs Nap begins to SWAY and her earrings start to move from side to side. Her necklace starts to CLONK as she begins singing LOUDLY as well.

"Oakfield School,
　　Oakfield School,
We love being at Oakfield School,
　　Teachers and pupils at Oakfield
　　School ... are the BEST!"

The last NOTE she sings is SO **HIGH** it makes the windows **RATTLE** and my ears hurt.

(There are dogs around town that can hear **Mrs Nap's** singing.)

"Did you enjoy that song?" **Mrs Nap** asks us.

(We're still slightly in shock.)

Next she hands around the contents of the box. I get a wooden spoon and saucepan, **AMY** has the cheese grater and spoon, and Marcus gets two whisks.

scrape
tap
tap
tap

"We're using kitchen utensils and percussion instruments ... like THIS."

Mrs Nap demonstrates by using a spoon on the grater. If I'm honest, the noise is a bit annoying, but she is <u>SO</u> enthusiastic and TAPS AWAY while singing that tune again.

"This is ridiculous – a WHISK?" Marcus grumbles, then BASHES it on the table. He's not the only one making a noise. There's pans, more spoons and other kitchen items. Everyone starts to play with them straight away. I say "playing" but it's more like **NOISE.**

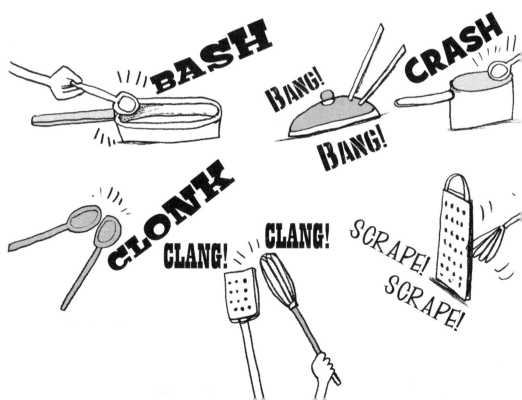

"UTENSILS DOWN! CLASS 5F. Solid – chopsticks on the table. Whisks, spoons and saucepans – stop playing with them, please!"

Mrs Nap calls out.

She picks up some wooden spoons and POINTS at Norman.

"Frying pan OFF your head!"

When we're all quiet (which takes a while), Mrs Nap shows us how to TAP OUT different rhythms that she wants us to copy, using her wooden spoons to demonstrate.

Eventually, we're all **TAPPING** out sounds that don't seem quite so bad.

Scrape
Tap

Tap

Ridiculous

$\textbf{O}$ur lesson is attracting a lot of attention from anyone who's passing our door. People keep PEERING in. It's putting some kids off playing in TIME, so $\mathbb{M}$rs $\mathbb{N}$ap tells us to ...

"... KEEP GOING! CONCENTRATE! DON'T LET ANYONE PUT YOU OFF!"

Just as the door opens and in walks Mr Keen.

"Is everything OK, Mrs Nap?" he asks.

"Yes, Mr Keen. We're having a WONDERFUL TIME making music with kitchen equipment!"

Mrs Nap explains.

"OF COURSE you are! Keep up the good work," Mr Keen tells us.

 He keeps BLINKING every time Mark Clump hits his saucepan lid.

We carry on **TAPPING** after he leaves. It takes a while for anyone to notice the BELL has gone for breaktime.

"Doesn't time FLY when you're having FUN?" Mrs Nap tells us. "Leave your instruments on the table, and this time try not to scrape your chairs..."

SCRAPE

SCRAPE

SCRAPE

I'm trying to explain to Derek what all the NOISE coming from our class was.

 "You were playing with wooden spoons?" Derek asks, sounding surprised.

"Yes! And **AMY** had a saucepan!" I tell him.

"I was using WHISKS. It was a bit ridiculous, if you ask me," Marcus chips in, using his FAVOURITE word again.

"Hey, I've got a silly game we can play if you want to," **AMY** suggests.

"What is it? I'm good at games," Marcus says confidently (as always).

Back in Class

Mrs Nap greets us all by SINGING our names really **LOUDLY** as we walk in.

♪ "Helloo, Tom Gates! Hi, Marcus and Amy! Sit down, Mark Clump! Hello, Florence!" ♪

(This is <u>NOT</u> something Mr Fullerman has EVER done.) Marcus keeps repeating (Fluffy bundle) to himself and trying not to laugh, which isn't working.

"It's not that funny, Marcus," I say as he keeps laughing. It looks like all the kitchen utensils are back in their box, so we're obviously doing something different. Mrs Nap is still singing.

"Everyone, SIT DOWN! Get ready – I want you to help me write ...

"... a **song!**"

Another high note takes us by surprise again.
"Think of an idea or subject – I'll write it down and then turn <u>your</u> ideas into a song.
Now, who's going to start?"

Mrs Nap is LOOKING around our class, and spots Marcus mumbling.

"Marcus – <u>you</u> look like you've got something to say?" she asks.

Marcus panics and BLURTS out ...

Errrr.

(I take it all back – fluffy bundle is FUNNY after all.)

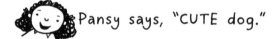

Mrs **N**ap writes "fluffy bundle" on the board, which **SPARKS** off lots of other odd suggestions from the rest of the class.

Pansy says, "CUTE dog."

"Spelling test," Indrani adds.

"Home!" Solid says.

"Ants," Mark Clump calls out.

 "This is going to be a tricky song to write," **M**rs **N**ap tells us.

Mrs Nap spends some time LOOKING at the words. Every time she TURNS her head, her earrings SWING around.

"Here we go – a short song based on YOUR words," Mrs Nap says, then begins to sing.

"There's a little cute dog,
It's a real fluffy bundle.
On the way home
It follows me closely.
I think it's the best.
This little dog ... is better than a spelling test!"

We give Mrs Nap a round of applause.

Then Mark Clump puts up his hand.

"Mrs Nap – you missed out the ANTS!"

"You're right. Well, why don't you put ANTS in your own songs? That's what I'd love you all to do now – write your own songs."

So that's what I did.

My song idea comes to me surprisingly fast.

BIG

Ants

Pants

Tiny pants

Tiny pants

The ants

    wore tiny pants,

   Then they found,

when they ran around,

Their pants weren't

   tiny enough.

(I think it's a classic.)

SILLY GAME 4

Can you find the pairs of ants in tiny pants.

(I'll start you off.)

SILLY BUG GAME 5

Spot the difference

Answers on page 238

SILLY BUG GAME 6

How many BUGS can you count?

(No answers for thi...
it's for fun.)

Celebrity
Sightings

There's a RUMOUR going around school that the :FAMOUS: actors Sacha Tosay and Rod Stable have been seen in Oakfield Town.

 They $STAR$ in the really popular SPY FILMS...

THE SPY AT NIGHT

DON'T SPY ON ME

THE SPY WHO DIDN'T LIKE ME

← My favourite
WHY SPY?

The SPY BOOKS are really good too.

Derek and I are waiting to go into school when Marcus comes ═══════ *RUNNING* over like he's got something really important to say.

Hey hey hey!

"GUESS WHAT HAPPENED TO ME?"

he shouts, then doesn't wait for us to answer.
"I saw Sacha Tosay and Rod Table!"

"Don't you mean Rod Stable?"
I correct him, but he ignores me.

"They were in the TOWN LIBRARY! I was
taking some books back and I SAW them.
AND they smiled at ME," he tells us, and is
almost jumping up and down.

More of our friends hear Marcus and want to know
what's going on.

"Did you say Sacha Tosay was in the LIBRARY?
Are you SURE?"

"Why would they be in there?" AMY wonders.

(It's a very good question.)

"I didn't ask them. I was too busy being EXCITED and SMILING!" Marcus says.

"Maybe they were getting books out of the library or taking some back?" Solid whispers.

 "Seriously? They're film stars – why would they be in the library?" AMY LAUGHS.

"Maybe ... they could be making a film?" Florence wonders.

"Did you see any cameras?" I ask Marcus.

 "No – but I wasn't looking for cameras."

"Are you SURE it was them? It seems a bit ODD they were in the library," Derek adds.

 (Marcus is getting a bit CROSS with us all asking questions.)

"Yes I **did** see Sacha Tosay and Rod Stable yesterday.

I'm going back to the library after school today to see if they are making a film - a <u>new</u> SPY film starring Sacha Tosay and Rod Stable."

Then a little kid walking past HEARS our conversation and joins in. "Hey, I know who you're talking about!"

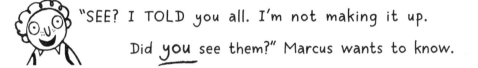

"SEE? I TOLD you all. I'm not making it up. Did <u>you</u> see them?" Marcus wants to know.

"Yes - on the POSTER at the BUS STOP. There's one for their new film.

I can't WAIT!" the little kid tells us.

(This is <u>NOT</u> what Marcus wants to hear.) The BELL goes for the start of school and he stomps off muttering to himself.

In class, Mr Fullerman hands out today's worksheet, which is all about writing stories in a DIARY style.

(Good for me.)

Marcus already has his hand up and is desperate to let Mr Fullerman (and the rest of the class) hear his news.

Sir Sir
Sir Sir
Sir
Sir
Sir
Sir
Sir
Sir

Here he goes.

"OK, Marcus, I can tell you're keen to share something with us."

"YES, SIR! I saw the REAL Sacha Tosay and Rod Stable at the town library yesterday after school."

Some kids say "WHOOOAA" as they are impressed - others LAUGH.

Mr Fullerman smiles. **"I see – how UNUSUAL to see famous people in Oakfield Town and in the LIBRARY too!"**

(He sounds like he's not sure it happened.)

Then I put up my hand. "Mr Fullerman, you're forgetting that **Teacup Tony and the Saucers** live in Oakfield Town – at the LEAFY GREEN OLD FOLKS' HOME. Well, **Teacup Tony** does and he was famous,"

I remind him.

"Not as famous as Sasha Tosay and Rod Stable," Marcus chips in, slightly annoyed.

Pansy puts up her hand.

"Sir, there's someone on my street who's FAMOUS for spending the longest time in a bathtub of baked beans!"

"Well, I take it back!" Mr Fullerman laughs. **"Perhaps that's what you could write about in <u>your</u> diary story today, Pansy?"** he suggests.

Marcus has already started his work. "It's like no one believes I saw them," he says, and glares in our direction.

"We do, Marcus. It's just funny that they were in the library," says AMY, and I agree.

"It's a bit like if they turned up in the local shop or playground. That would be unexpected, wouldn't it, Marcus?" I say to him.

"Whatever ... I'm going to write it all up in my diary story," Marcus mutters and gets busy.

AMY starts hers, and I'm left wondering what I can write about now.

Then it comes to me in a *FLASH.*

I'll write about the time Delia and I got stuck in the lift, and how she wanted to meet a famous author but couldn't. Then how <u>I</u> saved the day with my SPECTACULAR SIGN and all the very important things I kept in my bag.

I will get a lot of merits for this, I'm sure.

(And it's all true, of course.)

With my diary work all done, the bell goes for the end of the school day, Marcus leaves in a big ~~EE,~~ *HURRY.*

"I'm going back to the LIBRARY!" he tells us.

"If you see any other mega film stars, Marcus, let us know!" **AMY** calls after him.

"I WILL! I'm not making it up..." he shouts back. Derek and I had planned to head to the park and the shop on the way home. But now we're both curious to see if Marcus was making it all up.

"We might as well go - we could always get out a book," Derek suggests.

"Good point. Or we might be too busy hanging out with all the FAMOUS people - and Marcus," I joke.

"True," Derek LAUGHS.

On the way, we walk past the POSTER at the bus stop for the new spy film and stop for a closer look. "Nice poster. I've seen a few of those around town,"

Derek tells me.

"Maybe that's how the rumour started in the first place?" I wonder.

"The little kid saw the poster," Derek remembers.

"Marcus wasn't happy," I remind him, then take out my pocket money and check how much I have to spend.

Not much, but it's better than nothing.

After a good think, we settle on two **FRUIT LOLLIES,** then head off to the park.

"How long can you make your lolly last for?"

Derek wants to know.

"Not long – I've already taken a bite from the top and the bottom," I say.

"Let's see if we can make them last all the way to the park," says Derek.

"OK – and don't walk on any cracks in the pavement, either," I suggest.

This takes all our concentration. We do it though, and finish our lollies at the same time.

It's a lot easier to play in the park when you're not holding a lolly.

"What do you think Marcus is doing now?"
Derek asks me on the swing.

"Annoying someone – or looking for famous people."
I LAUGH.

"Or both," Derek adds.

After the park,
we head to the library,
which is pretty quiet (as normal).
The librarian tells us they're closing early today,
so we don't have much time. But that's OK.
"No sign of Marcus," Derek says.

"Or anyone else," I tell him.
I find a SPY book I wanted to
get out and Derek grabs a book
on snakes. We have a quick read
before the library closes.

"I'm going to show this
book to Mark Clump. He has a
pet snake," Derek reminds me.

When we get home, I draw a picture of a snake and show it to Derek from my window.
Derek does a picture of Mr Fullerman, which makes me LAUGH.

We've arranged to go and see the SPY film at the weekend and I can't WAIT!

At least then I'll be able to tell Marcus we HAVE seen Sacha Tosay and Rod Stable for real then. It might stop him from going ON about them.

$\mathbb{A}$t school the next day, Marcus can't WAIT to show me and AMY THIS photo.

"I **TOLD** YOU! They were still filming at the library, SEE – I don't know HOW you missed them!" he tells us smugly.

Nice!

Wow!

Smug

I don't know, either.

To be fair to Marcus – it's a really good picture and he does look very happy. I would be too.

Derek and I STILL can't work out why we didn't see them. It's a TOTAL MYSTERY.

(Marcus will remind us about it for ever.

I'd probably do the same.)

Homework Meter

When **Mr Fullerman** hands out homework, he tries to make it sound REALLY exciting. As if it's the one thing we're all really **THRILLED** to do.

He says things like,

 "Have I got a BIG treat for you ALL!"

"You're going to LOVE this!"

 **"I BET you can't WAIT to see what I've got for you to do today."**

Here's my "THRILLED" face. →

(184)

This is what Mr Fullerman gave me for my homework this week.

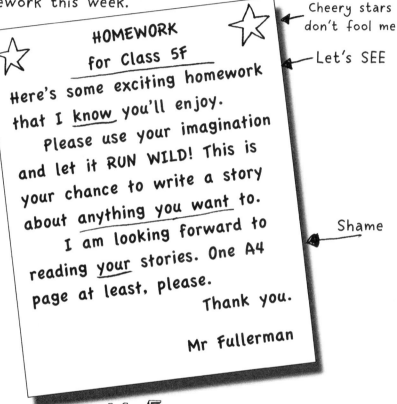

HOMEWORK
for Class 5F

Here's some exciting homework that I _know_ you'll enjoy.
Please use your imagination and let it RUN WILD! This is your chance to write a story about _anything you want_ to.
I am looking forward to reading _your_ stories. One A4 page at least, please.
Thank you.

Mr Fullerman

Cheery stars don't fool me

—Let's SEE

Shame

Mr Fullerman added the bit about how <u>long</u> it's supposed to be to stop kids doing things like this: "Once upon a time, there was a GIANT who got really BIG, then died. THE END."

(I've tried that before too!)

I HAVE to get a few more MERITS for my work because THEN I can get a **RED BADGE.**

Mr Fullerman has three colours of badge that he gives out if you've done something REALLY well.

RED BADGE if you've got lots of merits or you've been AMAZING.

BLUE BADGE for anything spectacular in sports or active stuff, dancing, music, that kind of thing.

GREEN BADGE for excellent environmental work, recycling projects or things like growing a HUGE sunflower. (Not as easy as it sounds.) I'm SO close to getting a RED badge, that's why this story is IMPORTANT.

The trouble is, I've been in my room  staring at a BLANK page for ages. The BLANK paper seems to be staring back at me.

Still staring...

I do a few doodles while I'm trying to think
of a story to write...

And then I get an IDEA!

Delia's
/ sunglasses

HomeWork

Mr Fullerman and anyone else who's reading my story: if these characters REMIND you of someone in REAL LIFE – it's just a weird coincidence.

The Sister Who Lost Her Smile

← Smil

by Tom Gates

There once was a really talented boy called ~~Tom~~ Tim who lived with his mum and dad and his **EXTREMELY** grumpy sister ~~Delia~~ Telia ... in the land of Fieldoak.

Their house was nice and large and quite fancy.

Tim had everything he wanted (apart from a dog).

 ←sad

TELIA on the other hand NEVER seemed that CHEERFUL.

Telia

(Mum and Dad said it was because she was a teenager, but I'm not so sure.)

One day Telia was complaining about having to look after her wonderful brother Tim (who was a JOY to be around, everyone said so). Telia's face was like **THUNDER.**

"Do I have to? I don't want to waste a minute of my precious time," she grumbled.

Mum and Dad shook their heads. How had they raised such a grumpy daughter? Especially when their son was such a DELIGHT! Then, while Telia was still frowning and FURIOUS, a big gust of wind ...

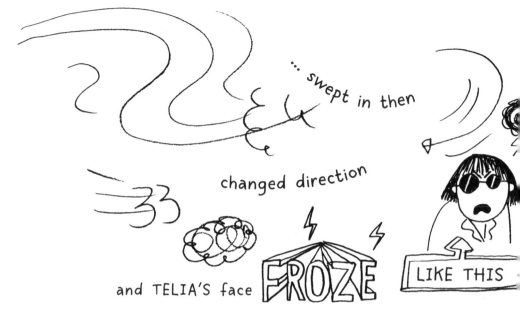

... swept in then

changed direction

and TELIA'S face FROZE LIKE THIS

She got stuck with a grumpy mush (face).

At first no one noticed, as that was her normal expression. But after a few days even Telia realized something was UP (or down, in the case of her mouth).

"This programme's HILARIOUS, isn't it, Telia?" Tim asked her while they were watching TV.

Telia just stared blankly.

"I think my smile's gone.

How can I get it back?"

"You might have to WAIT for the wind to change, and that could take a while," Tim told her because he was SMART and knew a lot of things.

Mum and Dad were worried that Telia would be stuck like that for ever.

"What happens if the wind doesn't change?" Dad said.

"We might NEVER see Telia's happy, smiling face again!" Mum replied DRAMATICALLY.

"I don't think I've ever seen it?" Tim pointed out.

"**W**hat are we going to do?"
Mum wondered.

"We could offer a **PRIZE** for anyone
who can make Telia smile again," said Dad.

"Good idea - but it will HAVE to be something
special - otherwise WHY BOTHER?" Tim said.

 "EXCUSE ME! I <u>AM</u>
here, you know,"
snapped Telia.

Whoops.

Mum and Dad set off to tell the whole of Fieldoak
Town about Telia's missing smile. They put up posters
and offered CASH and some CAKE if anyone
could help her get her smile back.

MISSING
SMILE

CASH and CAKE
to anyone who
can find it.

This could be an impossible task. But luckily, the people of Fieldoak Town were keen to help (and get the CASH and cake).

Cash

Cake

So it wasn't long before a QUEUE began to appear outside of the house.

"This looks promising," Mum told Telia. "We should let them come in and SEE WHO will bring back your smile," she added hopefully.

"Whatever," Telia grumbled.

Tim pulled up a chair to watch as he was sure this was going to take a while. Telia just looked ... miserable.

One by one, Dad let them see Telia. Some people really made an effort.

There were: Clowns

Slightly scary clowns ↓

Jugglers

Dogs in costumes

Flying dogs

Hot dog →

Comedians telling jokes

People who GURNED and pulled FUNNY faces

People wearing funny outfits

People doing silly dances

BUT NOTHING WORKED.

Telia's mouth didn't move at all.

Not one little bit.

"Who else is left?" Mum asked.

"That's it, I'm afraid. The FUNNIEST people in
the whole of Fieldoak have failed to get
Telia's smile back," Dad said ... sadly.

"The problem isn't <u>ME</u>, it's THEM!"

Telia said miserably.

"I'm going to be STUCK like this

 FOR EVER!"

The thought of Telia being even MORE grumpy wasn't great for anyone. Tim tried to look on the 'BRIGHT' side though.

 "Oh, well – at least we get to keep the money, AND more importantly ... the **CAKE**!

We should EAT some right now. Let's not waste any more time."

Tim was so keen to have a slice of cake, he *RAN* at speed and didn't see the small step until it was too late.

Tim tripped and flew through the air ...

... landing FACE FIRST in the cake.

At that EXACT moment, the wind changed
(which might have been a coincidence).
Telia's face began to QUIVER.
Her mouth moved from BIG FROWN to
a slight WOBBLE. The sight of Tim's face in the
cake made her SMILE.

Then she began to

LAUGH A LOT.

Telia hadn't laughed like this in YEARS.
Mum and Dad were delighted.

"Oh, what a WONDERFUL sight to see our
daughter SMILING and being happy again!"
Mum said.

"And it's all down to our BRILLIANT
SON, TIM!" Dad added.

Even Telia had forgotten how much she enjoyed
laughing at the misfortune of others.

(Tim, in this case...) →

Dad helped to clean Tim up and then they all managed to have some cake. Even if it was a bit

SQUASHED.

"I'm glad Telia found my trip FUNNY and that she's got her smile back," Tim said, as he was the best brother ever who always put other people FIRST. Because he was so good, Tim was allowed to use the money and BUY the DOG he'd always wanted. Telia wasn't happy about it at all, but then she was always grumpy about everything.

(So no change there, then.)

Once the dog arrived, she didn't smile again for a while.

(It had nothing to do with the wind changing.)

Tim wasn't bothered at **ALL** because he had a DOG!

And everyone lived happily ever after.

(Almost.)

THE END

Note for

Mr Fullerman.

I hope you're SUPER impressed that
I have written such a LONG story,
which I think deserves a LOT

of merits.

Space for merits

Eight
delicious
cakes

9

Nasty Nibbles

As soon as I walk through the door, I shout,

"HELLOOO, I'm HOME!"

in a funny voice.

No one answers.

This is GREAT news. That means Delia's still out, Mum's not back from work, and Dad must be in his shed working. I take a peek out of the kitchen window and I can see he's there talking on the phone.

EXCELLENT!

This give me plenty of time to help myself to some of that caramel ice cream that I KNOW is in the freezer.

Just a few scoops off the top - no one will notice.

Dad bought it when he stopped in the garage the other day.

I looked after it and wanted to eat some in the car. I'd found a spoon in my bag, so I was all SET.

"No, Tom – you can't eat ice cream straight from the TUB in the car!" Dad told me. (I actually <u>could</u> - but Dad made me wait until we got home.)

He took the ice cream from my warm hands and put it in the freezer. "It's starting to melt, Tom. We'll have it later," he said.

I couldn't stop THINKING about the caramel ice cream. It felt like it was going to be a long time before I could have some. It was only when Derek and Norman came round for a band practice that I forgot about it ...

... for a while,
while we practised
a few songs.

<u>BUT</u> as soon as they left, the

ICE CREAM popped

back into my head again.

The problem with this kind of ice cream is that you
can't just take a SNEAKY SCOOP

from the freezer. You have to leave it to go

SOFT first. I make sure no one's

around, then I take out the caramel

ice cream and put it by the window, where there's a

nice bit of SUNSHINE that will soften it

up quickly.

(It's a good plan.)

I whisper ... "Melt, melt, melt..." to hurry it up.  S T A R I N G at the ice cream doesn't *SPEED* it up. It makes sense to leave it for a few minutes while I ——— HOP on to the sofa and watch TV.

Being on my own means I can s p r e a d myself out and hold on to the remote control.

It's **BRILLIANT**.

I catch up on a few episodes of the CRAZY FRUIT BUNCH. They're so FUNNY. It's only after the THIRD one comes on that I remember.

"OH NO ... the ice cream!"
Which has only gone and melted ...

EVERYWHERE.

The lid of the carton has fallen off and all the caramel
ice cream has poured out over the kitchen floor.

It's a BIG, STICKY MESS.

"Awww, what a waste!"

Looking inside the carton, I manage to spoon
out the last tiny bit from right at the bottom.
It's delicious. Then I do my best to wipe
up the melted ice cream with a TON of
kitchen paper. It's still a bit sticky.

As I'm wondering what to do with the now
EMPTY ice cream carton, I hear the front door
SLAM and Mum say,

"I'm HOME!"

Uh-oh...

Mum will think I ate it ALL.

I'm not supposed to help myself either. I look round for somewhere to hide it.

I can't put it back in the freezer and the bin's too FULL.

Then I **PANIC** and *HURL* the carton into the garden, where it lands in a flowerbed.

Dad thinks I'm waving at him and waves back.

I smile and try to look relaxed just as Mum walks in.

"There you are, Tom – it's such a nice day I thought we should eat dinner in the garden tonight."

"Great idea, Mum!" I smile.

I'm just about to answer when Delia walks in and heads STRAIGHT TOWARDS

Uh-oh!

THE FREEZER!

"DELIA, what are you doing?" I shout, because I don't want her to see the EMPTY space where the ice cream **WAS.**

"Why do you want to know?"
she asks, sounding annoyed already.

Then <u>Dad</u> comes in and says, "Hi, you two. Thanks for waving at me, Tom – that was nice!"
(I keep quiet.)

"We're thinking of having dinner outside tonight, Frank," Mum tells him.

"Great! Hey, Tom – we can have some of that caramel ice cream for afters," Dad reminds me.
(This is getting awkward.)

  Huh...

ot forgetting that Delia is still LOOMING
towards the freezer. I try and stand in front of
her and casually stop to YAWN.

"Tom, do you mind? I need to
look at the calendar," Delia
says crossly.

"Oh! Well, that's OK then."
(She's not looking in the freezer.)
I let Delia pass and even SMILE at her.

"Why is it all sticky around here? Pass
me the kitchen roll, Tom," Mum asks.

"Errrr, it's all gone," I say and head
quickly out to the garden to ESCAPE and
make sure the ice cream carton is safely HIDDEN.

Dad gives me a job before I go.
"Take these out to the table, Tom!"

And another job ...

... then one more.

(Eating outside is a LOT of bother,

if you ask me.)

I don't even have enough time to properly
check the ice cream carton is still hidden before
Mum and Dad come and join me.

"I've put the chicken pie in the oven,

so it just needs to heat up," Mum says

and I immediately

LEAP FOR JOY. YES!

"Chicken pie is my FAVOURITE!" I shout.

"That and caramel ice cream. What a TREAT!"
Dad adds and I stop jumping.

Delia arrives once everything's done and takes the seat I wanted.

"Let's all sit down. The pie won't be long,"

    Mum suggests.

Out of the corner of my eye, I can see a little bit of the carton and LOADS of bugs that have started to FLY around it.

    I REALLY HOPE no one notices.

"There's a lot of **BUGS** and flies buzzing around over there," Delia says.

(Aghhhhhh!)

"Oh, yes – so there is. I wonder what's attracting them?" Dad wonders.

"I hope it's not a NEST of some kind," Mum adds.

(This isn't going well.)

I go and investigate before anyone else does, and make sure I hide the empty carton a little better.

"Be careful, Tom, you don't want to get bitten or make the bugs angry," Mum tells me.

"We wouldn't want that," Delia says, not sounding like she means it at all.

Trying not to let anyone SEE, I go over to
the flowerbed and give the carton a really
BIG KICK to push it further away.
But it gets stuck on the end of my SHOE and the
bugs go **WILD.**

"What are you doing, Tom?" Dad calls out.
            "Nothing!"
        I say and SHAKE my shoe.

Somehow I manage to

FLICK the carton right up in the air ...

219

... and it only goes and LANDS on my HEAD!

Straight away, the bugs start biting me.

"Stop messing around, Tom! Come and sit down, will you?" Mum tells me.

"I don't want those flies near me, Tom – stay there," Delia says, not helping at all.
I CLOSE my eyes to stop the BUGS bothering my face, then in one SLICK move, I swipe the carton OFF my head, SPIN round and try and CHUCK it back into the flowerbed ...

... or not.

OOOOPPPS

"TOM!" Delia shouts
before ducking out of the way. Dad manages to
catch the carton that's flying towards him.

"What's an empty ice cream carton doing in the
garden?" Mum wants to know. Delia and Dad are
LOOKING at me.

"I can explain - it's <u>not</u> what you think," I manage
to say, before the bugs go crazy and we all have to
go inside.

Bitey bugs

THE GOOD NEWS

Mum and Dad aren't as CROSS as I thought they'd be after I re-enact the whole melted ice cream story. "I just wanted a quick TASTE to make sure it was nice," I say.

"That was very good of you, Tom," Mum LAUGHS. Dad thinks we should get some more for later, which I AGREE with (I promise not to help myself again).

THE BAD NEWS

We're all so busy talking about ice cream that the chicken pie BURNS. "Pasta OK for everyone?" Mum asks. It's not that it's a bad swap, I just MISS chicken pie. There's more bad news for ME though – as it looks like I'm the ONLY one in the family who the BUGS found tasty. Dad dabs on some special cream, which helps. It's still annoying though.

But not as annoying as Marcus, when he keeps COUNTING all my bites at school the next day.

"One, two, three, four, FIVE, six,
SEVEN – oh, and there's another one –
EIGHT ... One more, NINE!"

"No need, Marcus."

Mr Fullerman mades us all *RUN*
around the school grounds to get rid of EXTRA
energy before we start our sponsored silence. (Now
my face is all RED.)

"OK, Class 5F, everyone ready?"
Mr Fullerman asks.

"YES, SIR..."

"So no talking – write down anything that you need
to say. Let's see how long you can last for!"

Five, four,
three, two, one...

S i l e n c e

As soon as Mr Fullerman says we can't talk,
the bites on my face start to "ITCH."

It's hard not to scratch them. Marcus holds up a
sign that doesn't help.

The ONLY way I'm going to get through the
SPONSORED SILENCE and not make a NOISE
is by:

✳ TRYING to THINK of something else (not itching)

✳ Ignoring Marcus

✳ Doing lots of really GOOD doodles.

I start drawing and it's a very good distraction.

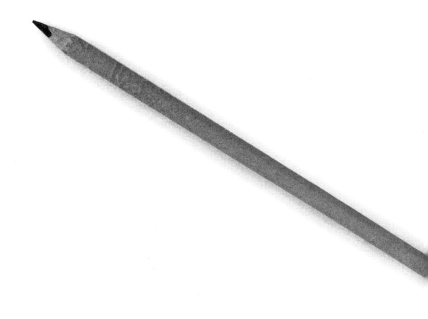

TEN

PETS I would like

Nice bunny

Medium dog

Friendly bear

Long dog

TEN TREMENDOUS TREATS

Banana to doodle on ↓

Milkshakes

I Crea (apart fr mint ch ch

Peas ↘ (not really)

CHEWS

FRUIT CHEW

A TOWER of chocolate raisins topped with a WAFER

WAFER

Cheesy PUFFS

POPCORN!

Choc bar of any kind

TEN TREMENDOUS

Expressions of Marcus, who's watching me draw.

Half an hour into our sponsored silence...

We managed to keep quiet for a little bit longer, until finally, Mr Fullerman said...

"WELL DONE, CLASS 5F! THE SPONSORED SILENCE IS OVER!"

Make a STAND-UP BUG

1. Take a piece of card from a cardboard box and draw a BUG.

Then colour it in and very CAREFULLY cut it out with scissors (ask an adult to help you).

2. Cut two extra pieces of card to use for the feet.

3. Cut them to the same size, then cut two SNIPS in the top in the same place on each foot. Now slot the bug body into the snips. The longer section should be at the back.

4. Slot the bug into the feet – longer section at the back to help it stand up.

5. Your bug should look like this when you stand it up. For the bug arms, cut out two more long, thin strips the same size and STICK them on the back of the bug with some sticky tape.

Bit
✓ of clay
or foil

6. For the antenna, use a paperclip and CAREFULLY unwind it. GET AN ADULT TO HELP as it can be tricky. Bend it into a CURVED shape. Now pop a bit of clay or scrunched-up foil on to the end and push both paper clips into the gaps of the card. OR tape them to the back of the bug's head.

7. Add a small book from thin card or paper, like in the picture, and STICK the bug's arms on to hold the book.

ANSWERS PAGE

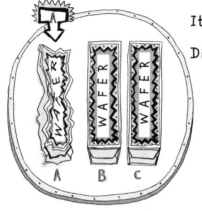

It's **A**.

Did you get it right?

(the teachers didn't)

Four Tremendous Tails
(pages 114-115)

Top left: chameleon
Bottom left: ring-tailed lemur
Top right: zebra
Bottom right: peacock

SILLY BUG GAME 5

Did YOU SPOT all the doodles from
The Brilliant World Of Tom Gates,
the first book in the series?

Previous Books

TOM GATES
EXCellent ExcuSeS
(and other good stuff)
BY LIZ PICHON

TOM GATES
EXTRA SPECIAL TREATS (not)
BY LIZ PICHON

TOM GATES
The BRILLIANT WORLd of TOM GATeS
BY LIZ PICHON

TOM GATES
A tiny Bit LUCKY
BY LIZ PICHON

TOM GATES
YES! NO. (Maybe...)
BY LIZ PICHON

TOM GATES
My School Project
FAMILY, FRIENDS and FURRY CREATURES
BY LIZ PICHON

TOM GATES
EPIC ADVENTURE (kind of)
BY LIZ PICHON

TOM GATES
Everything's AMAZING (sort of)
BY LIZ PICHON

TOM GATES
GENIUS IDEAS (mostly)
BY LIZ PICHON

TOM GATES
Absolutely FANTASTIC (at some things)
BY LIZ PICHON

NEW Tom Gates
is out in
OCTOBER
2021

Why the
Leg?

ONE VILE VILLAIN.
TWO COURAGEOUS CHILDREN.

The flying shoes of your most EPIC dreams.

Welcome to...

A laugh-out-loud, gadget-packed,
wedge-of-your-feet adventure like no other!

A *Sunday Times* children's book of the year.

"Full of Pichon's characteristic warmth, humour
and quirky illustrations" *The Bookseller*

Liz Pichon is one of the UK's best-loved and bestselling creators of children's books.

Her TOM GATES series has been translated into 45 languages, sold millions of copies worldwide, and has won the Roald Dahl Funny Prize, the Blue Peter Book Award for Best Story and the younger fiction category of the Waterstones Children's Book Prize.

In the ten years since THE BRILLIANT WORLD OF TOM GATES first published, the books have inspired the nation's children to get creative, whether that's through reading, drawing, doodling, writing, making, music or performing.

"I wanted to FILL the books with ALL the things I loved doing when I was a kid. It's just the best feeling ever to know children are enjoying reading the books, because I love making them. So thank you so much for choosing Tom Gates and keep reading and doodling!"

Alexa, 10, Loughborough

Josie, 8, Penarth

Ben, 10, Southampto

Emilia, 6, London

River, 10, Falmouth

Annalie, 10, Wokin

Wren, 6, Lancaster

Lilly, 8, Eastbourne

Cayden, 11, Fernd
Rhondda Cynon

Sebastian, 8, Telford

Camille, 9, Kent

Jess, 12, Derbyshire

Thomas, 8, Liverpool

Isla, 9, Silverstone

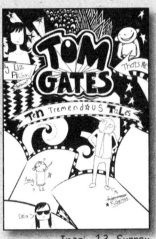
Inari, 13, Surrey

Aurora, 10, Surrey

Luca, 8, Eastbourne

Luca, 8, Eastbourne

Oenone, 12, Bedfordshire

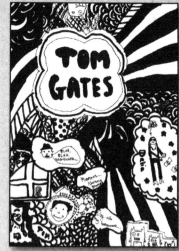
Sidra, 11, London

Joseph, 9, Stockport

Joshua, 9, Middlesbrough

Amira, 13, London

Harrison, 6, Hertfordshire

Annie, 7, Shropshire

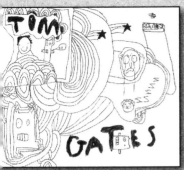
Leo, 7, Bristol

Evie, 12, Stockport

Ralph, 8, Chichester

Joseph, 9, Tonbridge

Zackaria, 8, Edinburgh

Ruari, 10, London

Jennifer, 12, Lincolnshire

Stanley, 10, Leigh on Sea

Oscar, 9, Eastbourne

Hammam, 11, Sale

Lana, 9, London

Sara, 11, London

Maya, 10, Grayshott

Oliver, 7, Shoreham by Sea

Joseph, 11, Balfron